THE
PRINCESS
AND THE
PIG

About the author and illustrator:

Jonathan Emmett was an architect before turning his hand to writing. Since then he has written many books for children – and won awards for them too. Jonathan's great grandfather was a shepherd and although there's no proof that his great grandmother was a princess, Jonathan is happy for people to call him *"Your Royal Highness"*, just in case.

Poly Bernatene has illustrated over sixty books for children in many countries all over the world. When he isn't busy illustrating, Poly works as a professor in the school in Argentina where he trained as an illustrator. Poly lives with his wife and two children, as well as a bookshelf filled with fairy tales.

For Caroline, who knows the sort of things
that happen all the while in books – J.E.

For my friend María Oms and her love for books – P.B.

First published 2011 by Macmillan Children's Books
This edition published 2013 by Macmillan Children's Books
a division of Macmillan Publishers Limited
20 New Wharf Road, London N1 9RR
Basingstoke and Oxford
Associated companies throughout the world
www.panmacmillan.com

ISBN: 978-1-4472-3533-0

Text copyright © Jonathan Emmett 2011
Illustrations copyright © Poly Bernatene 2011
Moral rights asserted

2 4 6 8 9 7 5 3 1

A CIP catalogue record for this book is available from the British Library.

Printed in China

THE
PRINCESS
AND THE
PIG

Jonathan Emmett

Illustrated by Poly Bernatene

MACMILLAN CHILDREN'S BOOKS

Not that long ago, in a kingdom not far from here, a farmer was travelling home from market with a cartload of straw.

The farmer was so poor that he didn't have a horse and had to pull his own cart. In the back of the cart lay a tiny pink piglet.

Nobody wanted to buy the piglet at market, but the farmer had taken pity on it. "I'll call you Pigmella," he decided, as this seemed like a good name for a pig.

It was a hot day and the farmer stopped to rest in the shade of a great castle. Far, far above him, on a high balcony, a queen was inspecting her new baby daughter.

The Queen was so rich that she had seven nannies and didn't have to look after her own child.

The Queen picked the baby out of her cot and held her at arm's length. "I'll call it Priscilla," she decided, as this seemed like a good name for a princess.

A moment later, a wet squelching noise came
from the baby's nappy, closely followed by an
awful smell. "Yuck!" shrieked the Queen, dropping
the baby and running off to find the royal nannies.

She left so quickly that she didn't notice she had
dropped the baby . . .

. . . over the edge of the balcony!

Down

down

down

went the baby,   into the farmer's cart!

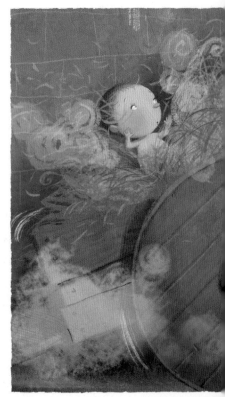

flew the piglet,   into the princess's cot!

up

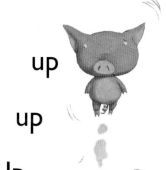

up

Up

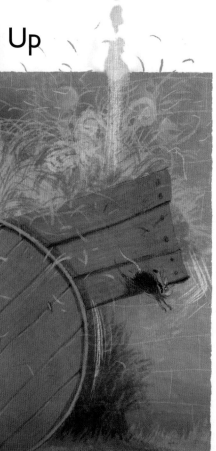

When the Queen returned and found the piglet lying where the baby should have been, she let out an even louder shriek and fainted into the nannies' arms.

The King thought he knew what had happened.

"A bad fairy has done this," he explained.
"The fairy wasn't invited to the Princess's
christening, so she's turned the baby into a
piglet to get her revenge. It's the sort of thing
that happens all the while in books."

Meanwhile, the farmer had returned home and was startled to discover a baby girl lying where the piglet should have been.

The farmer's wife thought she knew what
had happened.

"A good fairy has done this," she explained.
"The fairy knew how poor and honest we are and
how badly we want a child, so she's turned the
piglet into a baby. It's the sort of thing that happens
all the while in books."

And so, without a second thought, the baby
became Pigmella, the farmer's daughter.

And the piglet became Priscilla, the Princess.

It wasn't long before Pigmella was able to . . .

eat,

walk,

and dress, all
by herself.

And the farmer and his wife soon forgot that she
had ever been a pig.

Things were not so easy for Priscilla!

But the King and Queen never let anyone forget
that she was really a princess.

As Pigmella grew older,

she grew clever,

and beautiful,

and was
admired
by everyone
she met.

As Priscilla grew older,

she grew not
so clever,

and not so beautiful,

and was
avoided
by everyone
she met.

Then one day, the farmer's wife overheard some of the castle servants talking about the princess who had turned into a pig.

"It's just like what happened to Pigmella," she told her husband, "only the other way around."

The farmer soon guessed what had happened. "The Princess and the pig must have swapped places somehow," he explained. "It's the sort of thing that happens all the while in books."

The poor farmer and his wife were very unhappy. They loved Pigmella, but they knew they must return her to her rightful home.

Pigmella was also unhappy. She loved the farmer and his wife and did not want to live with anyone else.

But they were an honest family, so the next day they all went to the castle to see the King and Queen.

The King and Queen listened to the farmer's story . . .

But they didn't believe it! "What nonsense!" cried the Queen.

"Ridiculous!" laughed the King. "This girl may be clever and beautiful, but she does not look or speak like a proper princess."

The Queen thought she knew what was happening. "It's a trick," she declared. "This girl is just a farmer's daughter pretending to be a princess in the hope that she might marry a prince. It's the sort of thing that happens all the while in books."

And so Pigmella returned home with the farmer and his wife, where she married a young shepherd and lived happily ever after — and never once wished that she'd been a princess.

And Priscilla also got married — to a handsome prince! Although he had to be talked into it.

"Priscilla was changed into a pig by a bad fairy," the King explained.
"But once you kiss her, the spell will be broken and she will turn back into a beautiful princess," added the Queen.
"It's the sort of thing that happens all the while in books," they assured him.

THE
FROG
PRINCE

But, unfortunately for the Prince . . .

. . . it's not the sort of thing that
happens in this particular book.